THE TOAD PRINCE

Rebecca Lisle

By the same author

Copper
Dogs Don't Do Dishes